This ^naughty book belongs to

For Polly and Sheila

OXFORD
UNIVERSITY PRESS

Great Clarendon Street, Oxford OX2 6DP.
United Kingdom

Oxford University Press is a department of the University of Oxford.
It furthers the University's objective of excellence in research,
scholarship, and education by publishing worldwide

Oxford is a registered trade mark of Oxford University Press
in the UK and in certain other countries

Text and illustrations © Richard Byrne 2014

The moral rights of the author/illustrator have been asserted
Database right Oxford University Press (maker)

First published in 2014

British Library Cataloguing in Publication Data
Data available

ISBN: 978-0-19-273728-1 (hardback)
ISBN: 978-0-19-273729-8 (paperback)

1 2 3 4 5 6 7 8 9 10

Printed in China

Paper used in the production of this book is a natural,
recyclable product made from wood grown in sustainable forests.
The manufacturing process conforms to the environmental
regulations of the country of origin.

Visit www.richardbyrne.co.uk

This book just ate my dog!

Richard BYRNE

WALKIES!

OXFORD

UNIVERSITY PRESS

Bella was taking her dog for a stroll across the page when . . .

. . . something very odd happened.

Bella's dog disappeared.

'Hello Bella.
What's up?'
said Ben.

'This book just ate my dog!'

Ben decided
to investigate.

But Ben disappeared too.

Help zoomed into sight . . .

. . . then vanished.

Things were getting ridiculous.

'I'll just have to sort this out myself,' thought Bella.

But . . .

**Sometime later
a note appeared.**

It read . . .

Dear reader,

It would be lovely if you could kindly HELP US!

Please turn this book on its side and SHAKE...

Bella
x

1. Turn book around

2. Shake

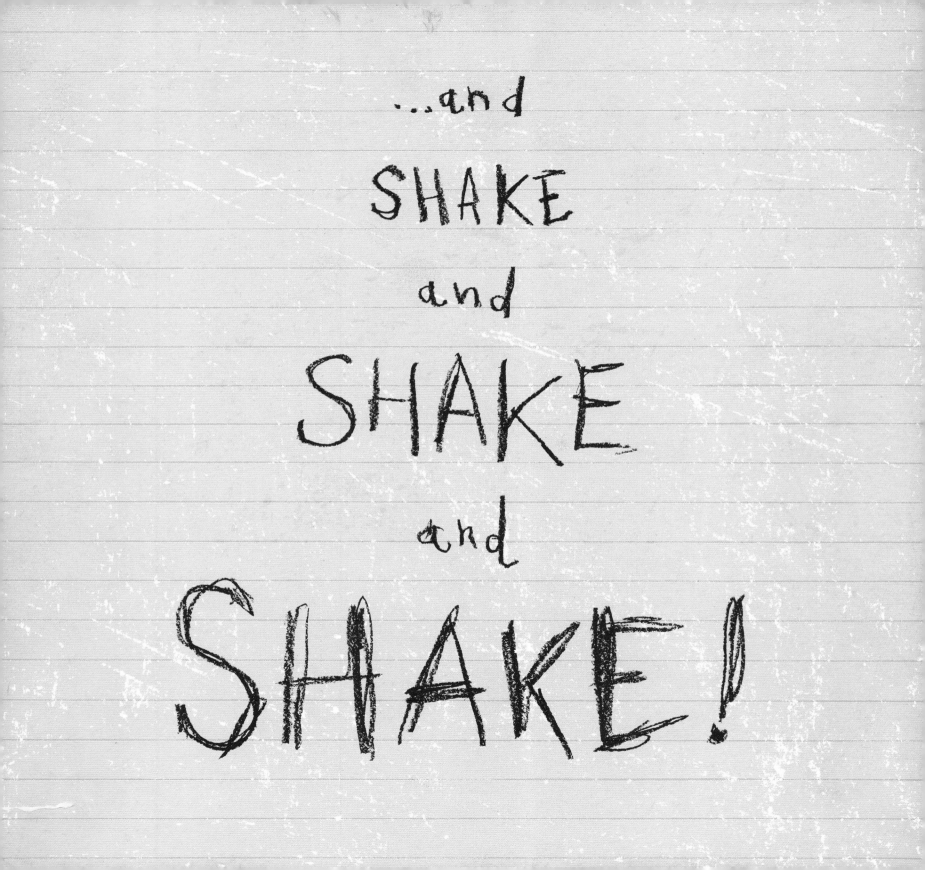

...and one last little wiggle. Thank you.

Bella x

Everybody reappeared . . .

. . . and things got back to normal.

Well, almost!

Dear reader,
Please tell this book to promise
not to be so naughty next time
you read it.
Thank you.
Bella
x